Henry Cuyler Bunner

Airs from Arcady and Elsewhere

Henry Cuyler Bunner

Airs from Arcady and Elsewhere

ISBN/EAN: 9783337058340

Printed in Europe, USA, Canada, Australia, Japan

Cover: Foto ©Andreas Hilbeck / pixelio.de

More available books at **www.hansebooks.com**

AIRS FROM ARCADY

AND ELSEWHERE

H. C. BUNNER

A Book of Verses underneath the Bough,
A Jug of Wine, a Loaf of Bread, and Thou
Beside me singing in the Wilderness—
Oh, Wilderness were Paradise enow !
— *Omar Khayyám*

CHARLES HUTT
CLEMENT'S INN GATEWAY .
LONDON
1885

TO BRANDER MATTHEWS:

BY THE HEARTH.

The night is late ; your fire is whitening fast,
　　Our speech has silent spaces, and is low ;
　　Yet there is much to say before I go —
And much is left unsaid, dear friend, at last.

Yet something may be said. This fading fire
　　Was never cold for me ; and never cold
　　Has been the welcoming glance I knew of old —
Warm with a friendship usage could not tire.

The kindly hand has never failed me yet,
　　And never yet has failed the cheering word ;
　　Nor ever went Perplexity unheard,
But ever was by thoughtful Counsel met.

The plans we made, the hopes we nursed, have fed
.　These friendly embers with a genial fire.
　　Not till my spirit ceases to aspire
Shall their kind light within my heart be dead.

Take these, the gathered songs of striving years,
　　And many fledged and warmed beside your hearth ;
　　Not for whatever they may have of worth —
A simpler tie, perchance, my work endears.

With them this wish : that when your days shall close,
　　Life, a well-used and well-contented guest,
　　May gently press the hand I oft have pressed,
And leave you by Love's fire to calm repose.

v

CONTENTS.

CONTENTS.

BOHEMIA.

ELSEWHERE.

ULTIMA THULE.

CONTENTS.

THE WAY TO ARCADY.

OH, what's the way to Arcady,
*   To Arcady, to Arcady;*
Oh, what's the way to Arcady,
*   Where all the leaves are merry?*

Oh, what's the way to Arcady?
The spring is rustling in the tree —
The tree the wind is blowing through —
   It sets the blossoms flickering white.
I knew not skies could burn so blue
   Nor any breezes blow so light.
They blow an old-time way for me,
Across the world to Arcady.

Oh, what's the way to Arcady?
Sir Poet, with the rusty coat,
Quit mocking of the song-bird's note.

How have you heart for any tune,
You with the wayworn russet shoon?
Your scrip, a-swinging by your side,
Gapes with a gaunt mouth hungry-wide.
I'll brim it well with pieces red,
If you will tell the way to tread.

Oh, I am bound for Arcady,
And if you but keep pace with me
You tread the way to Arcady.

And where away lies Arcady,
And how long yet may the journey be?

Ah, that (quoth he) *I do not know —*
Across the clover and the snow —
Across the frost, across the flowers —
Through summer seconds and winter hours.
I've trod the way my whole life long,
  And know not now where it may be ;
My guide is but the stir to song,
That tells me I can not go wrong,
  Or clear or dark the pathway be
  Upon the road to Arcady.

But how shall I do who can not sing?
  I was wont to sing, once on a time——
There is never an echo now to ring
  Remembrance back to the trick of rhyme.

'T is strange you cannot sing (quoth he),
The folk all sing in Arcady.

But how may he find Arcady
Who hath nor youth nor melody?

What, know you not, old man (quoth he)——
  Your hair is white, your face is wise—
  That Love must kiss that Mortal's eyes
Who hopes to see fair Arcady?
No gold can buy you entrance there;
But beggared Love may go all bare—
No wisdom won with weariness;
But Love goes in with Folly's dress—
No fame that wit could ever win;
But only Love may lead Love in
  To Arcady, to Arcady.

Ah, woe is me, through all my days
  Wisdom and wealth I both have got,
And fame and name, and great men's praise;
  But Love, ah, Love! I have it not.

There was a time, when life was new —
  But far away, and half forgot —
I only know her eyes were blue;
  But Love — I fear I knew it not.
We did not wed, for lack of gold,
And she is dead, and I am old.
All things have come since then to me,
Save Love, ah, Love! and Arcady.

Ah, then I fear we part (quoth he),
My way's for Love and Arcady.

But you, you fare alone, like me;
  The gray is likewise in your hair.
  What love have you to lead you there,
To Arcady, to Arcady?

Ah, no, not lonely do I fare;
  My true companion's Memory.
With Love he fills the Spring-time air;
  With Love he clothes the Winter tree.
Oh, past this poor horizon's bound
  My song goes straight to one who stands —
Her face all gladdening at the sound —
  To lead me to the Spring-green lands,
To wander with enlacing hands.

ARCADIA.

The songs within my breast that stir
Are all of her, are all of her.
My maid is dead long years (quoth he),
She waits for me in Arcady.

Oh, yon 's the way to Arcady,
  To Arcady, to Arcady;
Oh, yon 's the way to Arcady,
  Where all the leaves are merry.

O HONEY OF HYMETTUS HILL.

RONDEL.

[Dobson's Variation.]

O HONEY of Hymettus Hill,
    Gold-brown, and cloying sweet to taste,
Wert here for the soft amorous bill
    Of Aphrodite's courser placed?

Thy musky scent what virginal chaste
Blossom was ravished to distill,
O honey of Hymettus Hill,
    Gold-brown, and cloying sweet to taste?

What upturned calyx drank its fill
    When ran the draught divine to waste,
That her white hands were doomed to spill —
    Sweet Hebe, fallen and disgraced —
O honey of Hymettus Hill,
    Gold-brown, and cloying sweet to taste?

8

DAPHNIS.

I.

ERE the spring comes, we will go
   Where belated lines of snow
Lie in wreathlets chilly bright
Round the wind-flowers pink and white,
Trembling even as you, my own,
In my arms about you thrown;
Where pale sheets of ice-like glass
Fleck the marshland's greening grass;
Where beneath the budding trees
Dead leaves wait for April's breeze —
Chloë, Chloë, we will wander
Hither, thither, here and yonder.
Seeing you, the jealous Spring
Sure will haste a laggard wing,
   Though the upland plains are snowy,
Though the snow is on the plain —
   Chloë, Chloë, Chloë, Chloë!
But she answers not again.

II.

Chloë, lo! the Spring is here,
All the wintry walks are clear;
Prismy purple is the air
Round the branches brown and bare;
Purple are the doubtful dyes
Of the clouds in April's skies—
Come, and make last Summer stretch
Over half a year, and fetch
Smells of rose and violet
In the barren ways to set.
See, the wood remembering misses
Sweetness of our last year's kisses.
O'er the place where once we kist
Falls a vail of rainy mist —
    Tangled rain-sheets, wreathed and blowy —
There is weeping in the rain —
    Chloë, Chloë, Chloë, Chloë!
Ah! she answers not again!

THE HOUR OF SHADOWS.[1]

UPON that quiet day that lies
    Where forest branches screen the skies,
The spirit of the eve has laid
A deeper and a dreamier shade;
And winds that through the tree-tops blow
Wake not the silent gloom below.

Only the sound of far-off streams,
Faint as our dreams of childhood's dreams,
Wandering in tangled pathways crost,
Like woodland truants strayed and lost,
Their faint, complaining echoes roam,
Threading the forest toward their home.

O brooks, I too have gone astray,
And left my comrade on the way —
Guide me through aisles where soft you moan,
To some sad spot you know alone,
Where only leaves and nestlings stir,
And I may dream, and dream of Her.

ROBIN'S SONG.

U P, up, my heart! up, up, my heart,
   This day was made for thee!
For soon the hawthorn spray shall part,
  And thou a face shalt see
That comes, O heart, O foolish heart,
  This way to gladden thee.

The grass shows fresher on the way
  That soon her feet shall tread—
The last year's leaflet curled and gray,
  I could have sworn was dead,
Looks green, for lying in the way
  I know her feet will tread.

12

What hand yon blossom curtain stirs,
  More light than errant air?
I know the touch — 'tis hers, 'tis hers!
  She parts the thicket there —
The flowerèd branch her coming stirs
  Hath perfumed all the air.

The Springs of all forgotten years
  Are waked to life ànew —
Up, up, my eyes, nor fill with tears
  As tender as the dew —
I knew her not in all those years;
  But life begins anew.

Up, up, my heart! up, up, my heart,
  This day was made for thee!
Come, Wit, take on thy nimblest art,
  And win Love's victory —
What now? Where art thou, coward heart?
  Thy hour is here — and She!

A LOST CHILD.

Yᵉ CRYER.

HERE 'S a reward for who 'll find Love!
  Love is a-straying
    Ever since Maying,
Hither and yon, below, above;
  All are seeking Love!

Yᵉ HAND-BILL.

Gone astray — between the Maying
  And the gathering of the hay,
Love, an urchin ever playing —
  Folk are warned against his play.

How may you know him? By the quiver,
  By the bow he 's wont to bear.
First on your left there comes a shiver,
  Then a twinge — the arrow's there.

14

By his eye of pansy color,
   Deep as wounds he dealeth free ;
If its hue have faded duller,
   'T is not that he weeps for me.

By the smile that curls his mouthlet ;
   By the mockery of his sigh ;
By his breath, a spicy South, let
   Slip his lips of roses by.

By the devil in his dimple ;
   By his lies that sound so true ;
By his shaft-sting, that no simple
   Ever culled will heal for you.

By his beckonings that embolden ;
   By his quick withdrawings then ;
By his flying hair, a golden
   Light to lure the feet of men.

By the breast where ne'er a hurt 'll
   Rankle 'neath his kerchief hid —
What? you cry ; *he wore a kirtle?*
   Faith ! methinks the rascal did !

ARCADIA.

Here's a reward for who'll find Love!
Love is a-straying
Ever since Maying;
Hither and yon, below, above,
I am seeking Love.

Cryer: H. Bunner:
   Grub Street:
Cry's Weddings:
Buryings: Loſt
Childn, and right
cheaplie.
Ye IId Knocker.

MASTER CORYDON,

yᵉ Finder pray'd
to Bring her to

Petticoat Lane.

PHILISTIA.

DA CAPO.

SHORT and sweet, and we 've come to the end of it —
   Our poor little love lying cold.
Shall no sonnet, then, ever be penned of it?
   Nor the joys and pains of it told?
How fair was its face in the morning,
   How close its caresses at noon,
How its evening grew chill without warning,
      Unpleasantly soon !

I can't say just how we began it —
   In a blush, or a smile, or a sigh ;
Fate took but an instant to plan it ;
   It needs but a moment to die.
Yet—remember that first conversation,
   When the flowers you had dropped at your feet
I restored. The familiar quotation
      Was —" Sweets to the sweet."

Oh, their delicate perfume has haunted
  My senses a whole season through.
If there *was* one soft charm that you wanted
  The violets lent it to you.
I whispered you, life was but lonely:
  A cue which you graciously took;
And your eyes learned a look for me only —
    A very nice look.

And sometimes your hand would touch *my* hand,
  With a sweetly particular touch;
You said many things in a sigh, and
  Made a look express wondrously much.
We smiled for the mere sake of smiling,
  And laughed for no reason but fun;
Irrational joys; but beguiling —
    And all that is done!

We were idle, and played for a moment
  At a game that now neither will press:
I cared not to find out what "No" meant;
  Nor your lips to grow yielding with "Yes."
Love is done with and dead; if there lingers
  A faint and indefinite ghost,
It is laid with this kiss on your fingers —
    A jest at the most.

'T is a commonplace, stale situation,
  Now the curtain comes down from above
On the end of our little flirtation —
  A travesty romance; for Love,
If he climbed in disguise to your lattice,
  Fell dead of the first kisses' pain :
But one thing is left us now; that is —
      Begin it again.

GONE.

S HE stands upon the steamer's deck;
    The salt wind stings her cheek, goes by,
Comes back with kiss of foamy fleck,
    And sets her jaunty hat awry.

I sit beside the sea-coal glow,
    That with the night wanes less and less:
The room is dark — my heart beats slow
    With silence, loss, and loneliness.

JUST A LOVE-LETTER:

"'Miss Blank—at Blank.' Jemima, let it go!"
—*Austin Dobson.*

NEW-YORK, July 20, 1883.

DEAR GIRL:
        The town goes on as though
    It thought you still were in it;
The gilded cage seems scarce to know
    That it has lost its linnet;
The people come, the people pass;
    The clock keeps on a-ticking:
And through the basement plots of grass
    Persistent weeds are pricking.

I thought 't would never come—the Spring—
    Since you had left the City:
But on the snow-drifts lingering
    At last the skies took pity,
Then Summer's yellow warmed the sun,
    Daily decreasing distance—
I really don't know how 't was done
    Without your kind assistance.

23

Aunt Van, of course, still holds the fort:
  I've paid the call of duty;
She gave me one small glass of port —
  'Twas '34 and fruity.
The furniture was draped in gloom
  Of linen brown and wrinkled;
I smelt in spots about the room
  The pungent camphor sprinkled.

I sat upon the sofa, where
  You sat and dropped your thimble —
You know — you said you did n't care;
  But I was nobly nimble.
On hands and knees I dropped, and tried
  To — well, I tried to miss it:
You slipped your hand down by your side —
  You knew I meant to kiss it!

Aunt Van, I fear we put to shame
  Propriety and precision:
But, praised be Love, that kiss just came
  Beyond your line of vision.
Dear maiden aunt! the kiss, more sweet
  Because 't is surreptitious,
You never stretched a hand to meet,
  So dimpled, dear, delicious.

I sought the Park last Saturday;
  I found the Drive deserted;
The water-trough beside the way
  Sad and superfluous spurted.
I stood where Humboldt guards the gate
  Bronze, bumptious, stained and streaky—
There sat a sparrow on his pate,
  A sparrow chirp and cheeky.

Ten months ago! ten months ago!—
  It seems a happy second,
Against a life-time lone and slow,
  By Love's wild time-piece reckoned—
You smiled, by Aunt's protecting side,
  Where thick the drags were massing,
On one young man who did n't ride,
  But stood and watched you passing.

I haunt Purssell's — to his amaze —
  Not that I care to eat there;
But for the dear clandestine days
  When we two had to meet there.
Oh, blessed is that baker's bake,
  Past cavil and past question;
I ate a bun for your sweet sake,
  And Memory helped Digestion.

The Norths are at their Newport ranch;
  Van Brunt has gone to Venice;
Loomis invites me to the Branch,
  And lures me with lawn-tennis.
O bustling barracks by the sea!
  O spiles, canals, and islands!
Your varied charms are naught to me—
  My heart is in the Highlands!

My paper trembles in the breeze
  That all too faintly flutters
Among the dusty city trees,
  And through my half-closed shutters:
A northern captive in the town,
  Its native vigor deadened,
I hope that, as it wandered down,
  Your dear pale cheek it reddened.

I 'll write no more. A *vis-à-vis*
  In halcyon vacation
Will sure afford a much more free
  Mode of communication;
I 'm tantalized and cribbed and checked
  In making love by letter:
I know a style more brief, direct—
  And generally better!

SHE WAS A BEAUTY.

RONDEL.

SHE was a beauty in the days
    When Madison was President:
And quite coquettish in her ways—
    On conquests of the heart intent.

    Grandpapa, on his right knee bent,
Wooed her in stiff, old-fashioned phrase—
She was a beauty in the days
    When Madison was President.

    And when your roses where hers went
Shall go, my Rose, who date from Hayes,
    I hope you 'll wear her sweet content
Of whom tradition lightly says:
She was a beauty in the days
    When Madison was President.

CANDOR.

"I KNOW what you 're going to say," she said,
  And she stood up looking uncommonly tall;
  " You are going to speak of the hectic Fall,
And say you 're sorry the summer 's dead.
  And no other summer was like it, you know,
  And can I imagine what made it so?
Now are n't you, honestly?" "Yes," I said.

" I know what you 're going to say," she said;
  " You are going to ask if I forget
  That day in June when the woods were wet,
And you carried me "—here she dropped her head—
  " Over the creek; you are going to say,
  Do I remember that horrid day.
Now are n't you, honestly?" "Yes," I said.

" I know what you 're going to say," she said;
  " You are going to say that since that time
  You have rather tended to run to rhyme,

28

And "—her clear glance fell and her cheek grew red—
" And have I noticed your tone was queer?—
   Why, everybody has seen it here!—
Now, are n't you, honestly?" " Yes," I said.

" I know what you 're going to say," I said;
  " You 're going to say you 've been much annoyed,
   And I 'm short of tact—you will say devoid—
And I 'm clumsy and awkward, and call me Ted,
   And I bear abuse like a dear old lamb,
   And you 'll have me, anyway, just as I am.
Now are n't you, honestly?"

                    " Ye-es," she said.

"ACCEPTED."

W E were walking home from meeting, in the calm
old country street,
Where only a glimmer of moonlight through the arch
of the elms came down,
And wakening the twinkling shadows that played with
her little feet —
Playing hide-and-seek with the little feet that peeped
from beneath her gown.

There are things that a girl should n't think, and cer-
tainly should n't say —
But when she says them to you, the difference it
makes is queer.
And the touch of her hand on my sleeve seemed to ask,
in a soft, shy way:
"Can't you put your arm around me, or is n't it dark
enough here?"

A man does n't let that chance slip by him beyond
    recall;
  But I felt that it would n't do, after much con-
    sidering —
Her parents were just ahead, which did n't concern me
    at all —
  But her younger brother behind us — ah, that was a
    different thing!

We reached the dear old homestead the moon made
    tenderly white,
  And stood on the broad front porch, and all of them
    lingered to chat
Of how the soprano had sung and the parson had
    preached that night,
  And how the widow was out in another scandalous
    hat.

A look of appeal from me, and a wonderful glance from
    her,
  And we slipped away from the crowd, unnoticed and
    swift and still —
I think 't was the flower-beds I crossed; but I did n't
    care if it were —
  And she went back through the house, and we met
    at the window-sill.

At the window around the corner, with never a soul to see!—
And I stood on the grass below, and she bent down
from above,
And the honeysuckles were round us as she stretched
her arms to me,
And our lips met there in a new, new kiss — our be-
trothal gift from Love.

BOHEMIA.

.

A PITCHER OF MIGNONETTE.

TRIOLET.

A PITCHER of mignonette,
    In a tenement's highest casement:
Queer sort of flower-pot — yet
That pitcher of mignonette
Is a garden in heaven set,
    To the little sick child in the basement —
The pitcher of mignonette,
    In the tenement's highest casement.

POETRY AND THE POET.

[A SONNET.]

(Found on the Poet's desk.)

WEARY, I open wide the antique pane
    I ope to the air
I ope to
I open to the air the antique pane
  And gaze { beyond? / across } the thrift-sown fields of
    wheat, [commonplace?]
  A-shimmering green in breezes born of heat;
And lo!
And high
And my soul's eyes behold { a? / the } billowy main
Whose further shore is Greece   strain
                                again
                                 vain
[Arcadia — mythological allusion.— Mem. : Lemprière.]
  I see thee, Atalanta, vestal fleet,

And look ! with doves low-fluttering round her feet,

Comes Venus through the golden $\begin{cases} \text{fields of?} \\ \text{bowing} \end{cases}$ grain

(Heard by the Poet's neighbor.)

Venus be bothered — it 's Virginia Dix !

(Found on the Poet's door.)

Out on important business — back at 6.

YES?

IS it true, then, my girl, that you mean it—
The word spoken yesterday night?
Does that hour seem so sweet now between it
And this has come day's sober light?
Have you woke from a moment of rapture
To remember, regret and repent,
And to hate, perchance, him who has trapped your
Unthinking consent?

Who was he, last evening — this fellow
Whose audacity lent him a charm?
Have you promised to wed Pulchinello?
For life taken Figaro's arm?
Will you have the Court fool of the papers —
The clown in the journalists' ring,
Who earns his scant bread by his capers,
To be your heart's king?

BOHEMIA.

When we met quite by chance at the theater,
    And I saw you home under the moon,
I 'd no thought, love, that mischief would be at her
    Tricks with my tongue quite so soon;
That I should forget fate and fortune
    Make a difference 'twixt Sèvres and delf—
That I 'd have the calm nerve to impòrtune
    You, sweet, for yourself.

It 's appalling, by Jove, the audacious
    Effrontery of that request!
But you — you grew suddenly gracious,
    And hid your sweet face on my breast.
Why you did it I cannot conjecture:
    I surprised you, poor child, I dare say,
Or perhaps — does the moonlight affect your
    Head often that way

      *   *   *   *

You 're released! With some wooer replace me
    More worthy to be your life's light;
From the tablet of memory efface me,
    If you don't mean your Yes of last night.
But — unless you are anxious to see me a
    Wreck of the pipe and the cup
In my birthplace and grave-yard, Bohemia —
    Love, don't give me up!

A POEM IN THE PROGRAMME.

A THOUSAND fans are fretting the hot air;
  Soft swells the music of the interlude
Above the murmurous hum of talk subdued;
But from the noise withdrawn and from the glare,
Deep in the shadowy box your coilèd hair
  Gleams golden-bright, with diamonds bedewed;
  Your head is bent; I know your dark eyes brood
On the poor sheet of paper you hold there,
That quotes my verses — and I see no more
  That bald-head Plutus by your side.
                                    The seas
    Sound in my ears; I hear the rustling pines;
Catch the low lisp of billows on the shore
    Where once I lay in Knickerbockered ease
    And read to you those then unprinted lines.

BETROTHED.

IF when the wild and wintry weather
  Moans baffled round your warm home nest,
And swoops to pluck the light foam-feather
  From off the broad bay's heaving breast;
If then your fancy dim and dreamy
  One careless moment floats to me,
I hope, my sweet, you may not see me
    As others see.

Amid the crowd that glooms and glances—
  A silk sea, islanded with black,
And vexed with local storms of dances —
  I, making slow a sinuous track,
Bow, to the right, to Fan or Florry,
  Nod, to the left, to Nell. And she
Upon my arm, I should be sorry
    You knew knew me.

BOHEMIA.

The band above rolls rhythmic thunder
  Down on the whirl and glare below;
The dusty pine-floor pulses under
  The feet that balance to and fro.
Oh! dream of me that ills afflict me;
  Or dream about me not at all;
But do not let your dream depict me
      As at the ball.

With eyes that glisten, hands that tremble;
  With breasts that heave and cheeks that burn,
The gaudy groups disperse, assemble,
  And melt in other groups in turn.
Through flush of paint and frost of powder,
  I see a face or two I 've known,
That, rougeless, donned a carmine prouder
      For me alone.

If this were all, or worst, the whirling
  Among the other fools a fool —.
But when I stand my whiskers twirling
  Off by the lobby window cool —
And watch the dance where death's-heads grin to
  Death's-heads, bemasked, beflowered in vain;
See all—and then step reckless into
      That dance again!

BOHEMIA.

It were not sin to sin unthinking—
　　The drunken sense shall shrive the soul;
But when, withdrawing from the drinking,
　　I stand with cursèd self-control—
Ah, then, forgive me then, my pure one!
　　Poor, pettier deeds themselves defend;
For time and crime combine to lure one—
　　　　And there 's an end.

But, with hard eyes that plead no error,
　　To see my Life, sharp-waked from rest—
And then to lull the painted terror
　　To smirking slumber on my breast:
To see, beneath the rose and lily,
　　The black-rimmed eye, the sallow skin,
As clear as if even now the chilly
　　　　Gray dawn crept in.

Forgive me that!—Who touched my shoulder?
　　Oh, it was you, you ivory fan?
Dark domino, with eyes no bolder
　　Than should belong, by rights, to Nan.
What 's that? Aha, you 've caught me moping?
　　Fine me a bottle for the wrong—
A quart with silvered shoulders sloping—
　　　　Well, come along!

　　*　　*　　*　　*　　*　　*

BOHEMIA.

The whirl has changed to scattered revels,
  The glare to single scattered lights;
A hot and fluctuant draught dishevels
  The hair of Nancy Late-o'-Nights.
Her eyes are largish for their sockets;
  Champagney spray her satin flecks;
And I am feeling in my pockets
        For hat-room checks.

But, you, my fair, unconscious sleeping,
  No dream of day disturbs you yet;
The pale-faced star of love is peeping
  Through morning skies all misty wet.
I leave my partner, flushed and scornful
  Of etiquette, to seek the floor,
I fly, about that hour most mournful
        Of twenty-four.

When dark has lulled the day benighted
  Till dawn reveals the last caress,
And half apart they draw, affrighted
  Each at the other's ghastliness.
When Sleep, with face as blind and ashen
  As Death's, turns restlessly in fear,
As knowing, in some subtle fashion,
        That morn is near.

BOHEMIA.

With crisping snow the ground is whitened;
  The horses doze; the hackmen yawn,
Wearily waking; reins are tightened,
  The air is raw with coming dawn.
From the high porch I raise to Venus
  (Whose pallid radiance still endures)
My curse. The hall-door swings between us —
    My sleep and yours.

A thousand miles, a thousand ages
  Our dawns are parted, yours and mine.
For me, by slow and and sickly stages,
  The dull light climbs above the line.
You see, if ever dawn, surprising
  Your slumber, sets your spirit free,
Across white plains a clear sun rising
    Above the sea.

DEAD IN BOHEMIA.

IRWIN RUSSELL.

DIED IN NEW ORLEANS, DECEMBER, 1879.

SMALL was thy share of all this world's delight,
   And scant thy poet's crown of flowers of praise;
     Yet ever catches quaint of quaint old days
Thou sang'st, and, singing, kept thy spirit bright
Even as to lips the winds of winter bite
     Some outcast wanderer sets his flute and plays
     Till at his feet blossom the icy ways,
And from the snow-drift's bitter wasting white
   He hears the uprising carol of the lark,
     Soaring from clover seas with summer ripe —
     While freeze upon his cheek glad, foolish tears.
Ah! let us hope that somewhere in thy dark,
   Herrick's full note, and Suckling's pleasant pipe
     Are sounding still their solace in thine ears.

ELSEWHERE.

HOLIDAY HOME.

WHEN the Autumn winds nip all the hill-grasses
       brown,
And sad the last breath of the Summer in town,
When the waves have a chill, with a spicing of salt,
That warms the whole blood like no mortal-brewed malt—
Then I slip the dull burdens of Duty's employ—
New London, New London, New London ahoy!

There the latch-string is out, there's a hand at the door,
There are kindliest faces so kindly before—
Ah, the song takes a lilt, and the words trip with joy,
For New London, New London, New London ahoy!

When the Winter lies white on the roofs of the town,
A sound's in my heart that no storm-wind can drown;
Through the mist and the rain, and the sleet and the
       snow,
My memory murmurs a melody low,
Like the swing of a song through the brain of a boy—
New London, New London, New London ahoy!

FORFEITS.

THEY sent him round the circle fair,
    To bow before the prettiest there.
I 'm bound to say the choice he made
A creditable taste displayed;
Although — I can't say what it meant —
The little maid looked ill-content.

His task was then anew begun —
To kneel before the wittiest one.
Once more that little maid sought he,
And went him down upon his knee.
She bent her eyes upon the floor —
I think she thought the game a bore.

He circled then — his sweet behest
To kiss the one he loved the best.
For all she frowned, for all she chid,
He kissed that little maid, he did.
And then — though why I can't decide —
The little maid looked satisfied.

IN SCHOOL HOURS.

A REAL ROMANCE.[2]

YOU remember the moments that come
 In a school-day afternoon:
When the illegitimate hum
 Subsides to a drowsy swoon?
When the smell of ink and slates
 Grows oppressively *warm* and thick;
Sleep opens her tempting gates;
 And the clock has a drowsy tick?

Forgetful of watch and rule,
 The teacher has time to think
Of a "recess" in life's long school;
 Of a time to "go out and drink".
At the spring where the Muse has sipped,
 And laurel and bay-leaf bloom —
And a contraband note is slipped,
 Meanwhile, across the room.

From a trembling hand it flies
    Like a little white dove of peace ;
And away on its mission it hies
    In an "Atlas of Ancient Greece."
And the sender hides her face ;
    For her eyes have a watery shine,
And saline deposits trace
    The recent tear-drop's line.

From the dovecote side it goes
    Across to the ruder half—
Where a large majority shows
    A suppressed desire to laugh.
But the boy that they dare not tease
    Receives the crumpled twist —
And the little hunchback who sees
    Only shakes an impotent fist.

The boy with a fair-curled head
    Smiles with a masculine scorn,
When the sad small ·note is read,
    With its straggling script forlorn :
" *Charley, wy is it you wont*
    Forgiv me laughfing at you ?
I wil kill my self if you dont
   · *Honest I will for true !* "

He responds : He is pleased to find
    She is wiser, at any rate.
He 'll be happy to ride behind
    The hearse. May he ask the date?
She reads — with a glittering eye,
    And the look of an angered queen.
This were tragic at thirty. Why
    Is it trivial at thirteen?

Trivial! what shall eclipse
    The pain of our childish woes?
The rose-bud pales its lips
    When a very small zephyr blows.
You smile, O Dian, bland,
    If Endymion's glance is cold:
But Despair seems close at hand
    To that hapless thirteen-year-old.

      *   *   *   *

To the teacher's ears like a dream
    The school-room noises float—
Then a sudden bustle—a scream
    From a girl—"She has cut her throat!"
And the poor little hunchbacked chap
    From his corner leaps like a flash—
Has her death-like head in his lap—
    And his fingers upon the gash.

'T is not deep. An "eraser" blade
    Was the chosen weapon of death ;
And the face on the boy's knee laid
    Is alive with a fluttering breath.
But faint from the shock and fright,
    She lies, too weak to be stirred,
Blood-stained, inky and white,
    Pathetic, small, absurd.

The cruel Adonis stands
    Much scared and woe-begone now ;
Smoothing with nervous hands
    The damp hair off her brow.
He is penitent, through and through ;
    And she—she is satisfied.
Knowing my sex as I do,
    I wish I could add : She died.

THE WAIL OF THE "PERSONALLY CONDUCTED."

CHORUS HEARD ON THE DECK OF A SAGUENAY STEAM-BOAT.

INTEGRAL were we, in our old existence;
  Separate beings, individually:
Now are our entities blended, fused and foundered—
  We are one person.

We are not mortals, we are not celestials,
We are not birds, the upper ether cleaving,
We are a retrogression toward the monad:
  We are Cook's Tourists.

All ways we follow him who holds the guide-book;
All things we look at, with bedazzled optics;
Sad are our hearts, because the vulgar rabble
  Call us the Cookies.

ELSEWHERE.

Happy the man who, by his cheerful fireside,
Says to the partner of his joys and sorrows :
"Anna Maria, let us go to-morrow
      Out for an airing."

Him to Manhattan, or the Beach of Brighton,
Gaily he hieth, or if, fate-accursèd,
Lives he in Boston, still he may betake him
      Daown to Nantasket.

Happy the mortal free and independent,
Master of the mainspring of his own volition !
Look on us with the eye of sweet compassion :
      We are Cook's Tourists.

A CAMPAIGN TORCH.

I BLAZED like a meteor through the night
  In the great parade of the great campaign,
A smoke-tailed comet of yellow light
  I wavered and sputtered through wind and rain.
High over the surging crowd I tossed,   .
  A beacon of battle, flickering free ;
And now the contest is gained and lost,
  And victor and victim are one to me.

Ah, never again shall my dinted sides
  Ring responsive when, sharp and clear,
Comes up from the surging human tides
  The rousing sound of the party cheer.
Ah, never again shall my oily blaze
  Blow hither and thither, and fail and flare,
When a thousand masculine marchers raise
  Their " TIGAH ! " rending the midnight air.

And never again shall that bright blaze sink,
  When a sudden silence comes over the crowd ;
When procession and people, pausing, think,
  And even a heart-beat seems too loud.
When amid the revel of fire and noise
  Comes a thought of the days that were dull and dread,
And through these avenues marched the " Boys "
  Who to-day are heroes — or heroes dead.

When the fingers that hold me grip more slack,
  When the rabble ceases, a space, to rave ;
And men's minds travel a score years back,
  And the faces I light grow suddenly grave ;
When only the sound of the halting feet
  Like a vanishing rain-fall patters past,
With a muffled fall away down the street,
  And the thundering music stops at last ;

When even the buncombe orator, high
  On the flag-draped stand, as he looks around
Finds his breath come short and his throat grow dry,
  While his saw-edged voice has a husky sound ;
Feeling, for once in his life, afraid ;
  Remembering — ay, he remembered then !
That statecraft is not a tricky trade,
  That he deals with the honor and hopes of men.

ELSEWHERE.

No more my spirit of flame shall thrill
  As then : no more shall it leap and play
When the moment's madness masters the will,
  And the roaring column marches away.

  *   *   *   *   *

No more ! By November's night-winds fanned,
  In the gusty lee of a Bowery porch,
You may see me lighting a pea-nut stand —
  The battered wreck of a Campaign Torch.

November, 1880.

HOME, SWEET HOME, WITH VARIATIONS.

BEING SUGGESTIONS OF THE VARIOUS STYLES IN WHICH AN OLD THEME MIGHT HAVE BEEN TREATED BY CERTAIN METRICAL COMPOSERS.

FANTASIA.

I.

THE ORIGINAL THEME, AS JOHN HOWARD PAYNE WROTE IT:

'MID pleasures and palaces though we may roam,
Be it ever so humble, there 's no place like home !
A charm from the skies seems to hallow us there,
Which, seek through the world, is not met with elsewhere.

Home, Home ! Sweet, Sweet Home !
There 's no place like Home !

ELSEWHERE.

An exile from home, splendor dazzles in vain!
Oh, give me my lowly thatched cottage again!
The birds singing gayly that came at my call!
Give me them! and the peace of mind dearer than all.

Home, Home! Sweet, Sweet Home!
There's no place like Home!

II.

As Algernon Charles Swinburne might have Wrapped it up in Variations:

['*Mid pleasures and palaces*—]

AS sea-foam blown of the winds, as blossom of brine
  that is drifted
Hither and yon on the barren breast of the breeze,
Though we wander on gusts of a god's breath shaken
    and shifted,
The salt of us stings and is sore for the sobbing seas.
For home's sake hungry at heart, we sicken in pillared
    porches.   ·
Of bliss made sick for a life that is barren of bliss,
For the place whereon is a light out of heaven that
    sears not nor scorches,
  Nor elsewhere than this.

ELSEWHERE.

[An exile from home, splendor dazzles in vain —]

For here we know shall no gold thing glisten,
  No bright thing burn, and no sweet thing shine;
Nor Love lower never an ear to listen
  To words that work in the heart like wine.
    What time we are set from our land apart,
    For pain of passion and hunger of heart,
Though we walk with exiles fame faints to christen,
  Or sing at the Cytherean's shrine.

[VARIATION : *An exile from home —*]

    Whether with him whose head
    Of gods is honorèd,
With song made splendent in the sight of men —
    Whose heart most sweetly stout,
    From ravished France cast out,
Being firstly hers, was hers most wholly then —
    Or where on shining seas like wine
    The dove's wings draw the drooping Erycine.

[Give me my lowly thatched cottage —]

    For Joy finds Love grow bitter,
    And spreads his wings to quit her,
    At thought of birds that twitter
      Beneath the roof-tree's straw —

Of birds that come for calling,
No fear or fright appalling,
When dews of dusk are falling,
Or daylight's draperies draw.

[*Give me them, and the peace of mind —*]

Give me these things then back, though the giving
Be at cost of earth's garner of gold;
There is no life without these worth living,
No treasure where these are not told.
For the heart give the hope that it knows not,
Give the balm for the burn of the breast —
For the soul and the mind that repose not,
O, give us a rest!

III.

As Mr. Francis Bret Harte might have Woven
it into a Touching Tale of a Western
Gentleman in a Red Shirt:

BROWN ò' San Juan,
  Stranger, I 'm Brown.
Come up this mornin' from 'Frisco —
  Be'n a-saltin' my specie-stacks down.

ELSEWHERE.

Be'n a-knockin' around,
  Fer a man from San Juan,
Putty consid'able frequent —
  Jes' catch onter that streak o' the dawn !

Right thar lies my home —
  Right thar in the red —
I could slop over, stranger, in po'try
  Would spread out old Shakspoke cold dead.

Stranger, you freeze to this : there ain't no kinder gin-
  palace,
Nor no variety-show lays over a man's own rancho.
Maybe it hain't no style, but the Queen in the Tower o'
  London
Ain't got naathin' I 'd swop for that house over thar
  on the hill-side.

Thar is my ole gal, 'n' the kids, 'n' the rest o' my live-
  stock ;
Thar my Remington hangs, and thar there s a griddle-
  cake br'ilin' —
For the two of us, pard — and thar, I allow, the heavens
Smile more friendly-like than on any other locality.

ELSEWHERE.

Stranger, nowhere else I don't take no satisfaction.
Gimme my ranch, 'n' them friendly old Shanghai
    chickens —
I brung the original pair f'm the States in eighteen-'n'-
    fifty —
Gimme them and the feelin' of solid domestic comfort.

    Yer parding, young man—
      But this landscape a kind
    Er flickers — I 'low 'twuz the po'try —
      I thought thet my eyes hed gone blind.

   *   *   *   *   *   *

    Take that pop from my belt!
      Hi, thar — gimme yer han' —
    Or I 'll kill myself—Lizzie!—she 's left me—
      Gone off with a purtier man!

    Thar, I 'll quit — the ole gal
      An' the kids — run away!
    I be derned! Howsomever, come in, pard—
      The griddle-cake 's thar, anyway.

IV.

AS AUSTIN DOBSON MIGHT HAVE TRANSLATED IT
FROM HORACE, IF IT HAD EVER OCCURRED
TO HORACE TO WRITE IT :

RONDEAU.

Palatiis in remotis voluptates
Si quæris   . . .
  —FLACCUS, Q. HORATIUS, *Carmina, Lib. V: 1.*

AT home alone, O Nomades,
  Although Mæcenas' marble frieze
    Stand not between you and the sky,
    Nor Persian luxury supply
Its rosy surfeit, find ye ease.

Tempt not the far Ægean breeze ;
With home-made wine and books that please,
    To duns and bores the door deny
          At home, alone.

Strange joys may lure. Your deities
Smile here alone. Oh, give me these :
    Low eaves, where birds familiar fly,
    And peace of mind, and, fluttering by,
My Lydia's graceful draperies,
          At home, *alone.*

V.

As it might have been Constructed in 1744,
Oliver Goldsmith, at 19, Writing the
First Stanza, and Alexander Pope,
at 52, the Second:

HOME! at the word, what blissful visions rise;
    Lift us from earth, and draw toward the skies!
'Mid mirag'd towers, or meretricious joys,
Although we roam, one thought the mind employs:
Or lowly hut, good friend, or loftiest dome,
Earth knows no spot so holy as our Home.
There, where affection warms the father's breast,
There is the spot of heav'n most surely blest.
Howe'er we search, though wandering with the wind
Through frigid Zembla, or the heats of Ind,
Not elsewhere may we seek, nor elsewhere know,
The light of heav'n upon our dark below.

When from our dearest hope and haven reft,
Delight nor dazzles, nor is luxury left,
We long, obedient to our nature's law,
To see again our hovel thatched with straw:
See birds that know our avenaceous store
Stoop to our hand, and thence repleted soar:
But, of all hopes the wanderer's soul that share,
His pristine peace of mind 's his final prayer.

VI.

As Walt Whitman might have Written all around it:

I.

YOU over there, young man with the guide-book, red-
bound, covered flexibly with red linen,
Come here, I want to talk with you; I, Walt, the Man-
hattanese, citizen of these States, call you.
Yes, and the courier, too, smirking, smug-mouthed, with
oil'd hair; a garlicky look about him generally; him,
too, I take in, just as I would a coyote, or a king, or a
toad-stool, or a ham-sandwich, or anything or anybody
else in the world.
Where are you going?
You want to see Paris, to eat truffles, to have a good time;
in Vienna, London, Florence, Monaco, to have a good
time; you want to see Venice.
Come with me. I will give you a good time; I will give
you all the Venice you want, and most of the Paris.
I, Walt, I call to you. I am all on deck! Come and loafe
with me! Let me tote you around by your elbow and
show you things.
You listen to my ophicleide!
Home!

Home, I celebrate. I elevate my fog-whistle, inspir'd by
the thought of home.

Come in ! — take a front seat ; the jostle of the crowd not
minding ; there is room enough for all of you.

This is my exhibition — it is the greatest show on earth —
there is no charge for admission.

All you have to pay me is to take in my romanza.

2.

1. The brown-stone house ; the father coming home
worried from a bad day's business ; the wife meets him
in the marble-pav'd vestibule ; she throws her arms
about him ; she presses him close to her ; she looks him
full in the face with affectionate eyes ; the frown from
his brow disappearing.

Darling, she says, *Johnny has fallen down and cut his
head ; the cook is going away, and the boiler leaks.*

2. The mechanic's dark little third-story room, seen in a
flash from the Elevated Railway train ; the sewing-
machine in a corner ; the small cook-stove ; the whole
family eating cabbage around a kerosene lamp ; of the
clatter and roar and groaning wail of the Elevated
train unconscious ; of the smell of the cabbage unconscious.

Me, passant, in the train, of the cabbage not quite so unconscious.

3. The French flat; the small rooms, all right-angles, unindividual; the narrow halls; the gaudy cheap decorations everywhere.

The janitor and the cook exchanging compliments up and down the elevator-shaft; the refusal to send up more coal, the solid splash of the water upon his head, the language he sends up the shaft, the triumphant laughter of the cook, to her kitchen retiring.

4. The widow's small house in the suburbs of the city; the widow's boy coming home from his first day down town; he is flushed with happiness and pride; he is no longer a school-boy, he is earning money; he takes on the airs of a man and talks learnedly of business.

5. The room in the third-class boarding-house; the mean little hard-coal fire, the slovenly Irish servant-girl making it, the ashes on the hearth, the faded furniture, the private provender hid away in the closet, the dreary back-yard out the window; the young girl at the glass, with her mouth full of hair-pins, doing up her hair to go down-stairs and flirt with the young fellows in the parlor.

6. The kitchen of the old farm-house; the young convict just return'd from prison — it was his first offense, and the judges were lenient to him.

He is taking his first meal out of prison; he has been re-
ceiv'd back, kiss'd, encourag'd to start again; his lungs,
his nostrils expand with the big breaths of free air; with
shame, with wonderment, with a trembling joy, his heart
too expanding.

The old mother busies herself about the table; she has
ready for him the dishes he us'd to like; the father sits
with his back to them, reading the newspaper, the newspaper shaking and rustling much; the children hang
wondering around the prodigal — they have been cau-
tion'd: *Do not ask where our Jim has been; only say you
are glad to see him.*

The elder daughter is there, pale-fac'd, quiet; her young
man went back on her four years ago; his folks would
not let him marry a convict's sister. She sits by the
window, sewing on the children's clothes, the clothes not
only patching up; her hunger for children of her own
invisibly patching up.

The brother looks up; he catches her eye, he fearful,
apologetic; she smiles back at him, not reproachfully
smiling, with loving pretense of hope smiling — it is too
much for him; he buries his face in the folds of the
mother's black gown.

7. The best room of the house, on the Sabbath only
open'd; the smell of horse-hair furniture and mahog-
any varnish; the ornaments on the what-not in the

corner; the wax fruit, dusty, sunken, sagged in, consumptive-looking, under a glass globe; the sealing-wax imitation of coral; the cigar boxes with shells plastered over; the perforated card-board motto.

The kitchen; the housewife sprinkling the clothes for the fine ironing to-morrow — it is Third-day night, and the plain things are already iron'd, now in cupboards, in drawers stowed away.

The wife waiting for the husband — he is at the tavern, jovial, carousing; she, alone in the kitchen sprinkling clothes — the little red wood clock with peaked top, with pendulum wagging behind a pane of gayly painted glass, strikes twelve.

The sound of the husband's voice on the still night air — he is singing: *We won't go home till morning!* — the wife arising, toward the wood-shed hastily going, stealthily entering, the voice all the time coming nearer, inebriate, chantant.

The wood-shed; the club behind the door of the wood-shed; the wife annexing the club; the husband approaching, always inebriate, chantant.

The husband passing the door of the wood-shed; the club over his head, now with his head in contact; the sudden cessation of the song; the temperance pledge signed the next morning; the benediction of peace over the domestic foyer temporarily resting.

ELSEWHERE.

3.

I sing the soothing influences of home.

You, young man, thoughtlessly wandering, with courier, with guide-book wandering,

You hearken to the melody of my steam-calliope.

Yawp!

ULTIMA THULE.

FORTY.

IN the heyday of my years, when I thought the world
    was young,
  And believed that I was old — at the very gates of Life—
It seemed in every song the birds of heaven sung
  That I heard the sweet injunction: "Go get thee a
    wife ! "

And within the breast of youth woke a secret sweet desire;
  For Love spoke in that carol his first mysterious word,
That to-day through ashen years kindles memory into fire,
  Though the birds are dead that sang it, and the heart
    is old that heard.

I have watched my youth's blue heavens flush to angry,
    brooding red,
  And again the crimson palsied in a dull, unpregnant
    gloom ;
I am older than some sorrows; I have watched by Pleasure
    dead ;
  I have seen Hope grow immortal at the threshold of
    the tomb.

Through the years by turns that gave me now curses,
    now caresses,
  I have fought a fight with Fortune wherein Love hath
    had no part;
To-day, when peace hard-conquered ripe years and weary
    blesses,
  Will my fortieth summer pardon twenty winters to my
    heart?

When the spring-tide verdure darkens to the summer's
    deeper glories,
  And in the thickening foliage doth the year its life renew,
Will to me the forests whisper once more their wind-
    learnt stories?
  Will the birds their message bring me from out the
    heaven of blue?

Will the wakened world sing for me the old enchanted
    song —
  Touch the underflow of love that, through all the toil
    and strife,
Has only grown the stronger as the years passed lone
    and long?
  Shall I learn the will of Heaven is to get me a wife?

The boy's heart yearns for freedom, he walks hand-in-
hand with pleasure;

Made bright with wine and kisses, he sees the face of Life;

He would make the world a pleasaunce for a love that knows
not measure;

But the man seeks Heaven, and finds it in the bosom
of his wife.

STRONG AS DEATH.

O DEATH, when thou shalt come to me
    From out thy dark, where she is now,
Come not with graveyard smell on thee,
  Or withered roses on thy brow.

Come not, O Death, with hollow tone,
  And soundless step, and clammy hand—
Lo, I am now no less alone
  Than in thy desolate, doubtful land;

But with that sweet and subtle scent
  That ever clung about her (such
As with all things she brushed was blent);
  And with her quick and tender touch.

ULTIMA THULE.

With the dim gold that lit her hair,
  Crown thyself, Death; let fall thy tread
So light that I may dream her there,
  And turn upon my dying bed.

And through my chilling veins shall flame
  My love, as though beneath her breath;
And in her voice but call my name,
  And I will follow thee, O Death.

DEAF.

AS to a bird's song she were listening,
   Her beautiful head is ever sidewise bent;
 Her questioning eyes lift up their depths intent —
She, who will never hear the wild-birds sing.
My words within her ears' cold chambers ring
   Faint, with the city's murmurous sub-tones blent;
   Though with such sounds as suppliants may have sent
To high-throned goddesses, my speech takes wing.

Not for the side-poised head's appealing grace
   I gaze, nor hair where fire in shadow lies—
For her this world's unhallowed noises base
   Melt into silence; not our groans, our cries,
Our curses, reach that high-removèd place
   Where dwells her spirit, innocently wise.

LES MORTS VONT VITE.

*L*ES *morts vont vite !* Ay, for a little space
    We miss and mourn them, fallen from their place;
  To take our portion in their rest are fain;
  But by-and-by, having wept, press on again,
Perchance to win their laurels in the race.

What man would find the old in the new love's face?
Seek on the fresher lips the old kisses' trace?
  For withered roses newer blooms disdain?
            Les morts vont vite !

But when disease brings thee in piteous case,
Thou shalt thy dead recall, and thy ill grace
  To them for whom remembrance plead in vain.
  Then, shuddering, think, while thy bed-fellow Pain
Clasps thee with arms that cling like Death's embrace:
            Les morts vont vite !

DISASTER.

A ROAR of voices and a tottering town,
  A dusty ruin of high walls crumbling down,

A wild, blind hurrying of men mad with fear,
Rushing from death to death — above, the clear,

Calm, pitiless, lurid orange of the sky,
Where one affrighted vulture dares to fly.

On either side an ocean's overflow;
And fume and thunder of hid fires below.

      *   *   *

Then, when the next morn breaks, fair, heartless,
    bland,
The young west wind strews a dead world with sand :

Follows the broad and jagged swath where Fate
Has mown a thousand corpses mutilate.

And on the writhen faces bends to see
Unspeakable fear, defiance, agony.

Sees life's vain protest turned to impotent stone,
Dumbly reproachful still, and sees, alone,

Smiling in death, serene, sweet, undistressed,
One woman with a cancer at her breast.

SEPTEMBER.

RONDEAU.

THE Summer 's gone—how did it go?
And where has gone the dogwood's snow?
 The air is sharp upon the hill,
 And with a tinkle sharp and chill
The icy little brooklets flow.

What is it in the season, though,
Brings back the days of old, and so
  Sets memory recalling still
    The Summer 's gone?

Why are my days so dark? for lo!
The maples with fresh glory glow,
 Fair shimmering mists the valleys fill,
 The keen air sets the blood a-thrill—
Ah! now that *you* are gone, I know
    The Summer 's gone.

THEN.

WHEN, moved by sudden strange desires,
  And innocent shames and sweet distress,
Your eyes grow large and moist, your lips
Pout to a kiss, while virgin fires
  Run flushing to your finger tips —
Then I will tell you what you guess.

THE APPEAL TO HAROLD.[3]

HARO! Haro!
  Judge now betwixt this woman and me,
    Haro!
She leaves me bond, who found me free.
Of love and hope she hath drained me dry —
Yea, barren as a drought-struck sky;
She hath not left me tears for weeping,
Nor will my eyelids close in sleeping.
I have gathered all my life's-blood up —
    Haro!
She hath drunk and thrown aside the cup.

Shall she not give me back my days?
     Haro!
I made them perfect for her praise.
There was no flower in all the brake
I found not fairer for her sake;
There was no sweet thought I did not fashion
For aid and servant to my passion.
Labor and learning worthless were,
     · Haro!
Save that I made them gifts for her.

Shall she not give me back my nights?
     Haro!
Give me sweet sleep for brief delights?
Lo, in the night's wan mid I lie,
And ghosts of hours that are dead go by:
Hours of a love that died unshriven;
Of a love in change for my manhood given:
She caressed and slew my soul's white truth,
     Haro!
Shall she not give me back my youth?

Haro! Haro!
Tell thou me not of a greater judge,
     Haro!
It is He who hath my sin in grudge.
Yea, from God I appeal to thee;

ULTIMA THULE.

God hath not part or place for me.
Thou who hast sinned, judge thou my sinning:
I have staked my life for a woman's winning;
She hath stripped me of all save remembering—
       Haro !
Right thou me, right thou me, Harold the King !

TO A DEAD WOMAN.

NOT a kiss in life; but one kiss, at life's end,
    I have set on the face of Death in trust for thee.
Through long years keep it fresh on thy lips, O friend!
    At the gate of Silence give it back to me.

THE OLD FLAG.

OFF with your hat as the flag goes by!
   And let the heart have its say;
You 're man enough for a tear in your eye
   That you will not wipe away.

You 're man enough for a thrill that goes
   To your very finger-tips —
Ay! the lump just then in your throat that rose
   Spoke more than your parted lips.

Lift up the boy on your shoulder, high,
   And show him the faded shred —
Those stripes would be red as the sunset sky
   If Death could have dyed them red.

The man that bore it with Death has lain
   This twenty years and more;—
He died that the work should not be vain
   Of the men who bore it before.

ULTIMA THULE.

The man that bears it is bent and old,
　　And ragged his beard and gray,—
But look at his eye fire young and bold,
　　At the tune that he hears them play.

The old tune thunders through all the air,
　　And strikes right in to the heart;—
If ever it calls for *you*, boy, be there!
　　Be there, and ready to start.

Off with your hat as the flag goes by!
　　Uncover the youngster's head!
Teach him to hold it holy and high,
　　For the sake of its sacred dead.

Evacuation Day, 1883.

FROM A COUNTING-HOUSE.

THERE is an hour when first the westering sun
   Takes on some forecast faint of future red;
When from the wings of weariness is shed
A spell upon us toilers, every one;
The day's work lags a little, well-nigh done;
   Far dusky lofts through all the close air spread
   A smell of eastern bales; the old clerk's head
Nods by my side, heavy with dreams begun
In dear dead days wherein his heart is tombed.
   But I my way to Italy have found;
     Or wander where high stars gleam coldly through
The Alpine skies; or in some nest perfumed,
   With soft Parisian luxury set round,
     Hold out my arms and cry " At last! " to you.

TO A HYACINTH PLUCKED FOR
DECORATION DAY.

O FLOWER, plucked before the dew
  Could wet thy thirsty petals blue—
Grieve not! a dearer dew for thee
Shall be the tears of Memory.

LONGFELLOW.

POET whose sunny span of fruitful years
 Outreaches earth, whose voice within our ears
Grows silent — shall we mourn for thee ? Our sigh
 Is April's breath, our grief is April's tears.

If this be dying, fair it is to die :
Even as a garment weariness lays by,
Thou layest down life to pass, as Time hath passed,
 From wintry rigors to a Springtime sky.

Are there tears left to give thee at the last,
 Poet of spirits crushed and hearts down-cast,
Loved of worn women who, when work is done,
 Weep o'er thy page in twilights fading fast ?

ULTIMA THULE.

Oh, tender-toned and tender-hearted one,
We give thee to the season new begun;
Lay thy white head within the arms of Spring—
Thy song had all her shower and her sun.

Nay, let us not such sorrowful tribute bring,
Now that thy lark-like soul hath taken wing:
A grateful memory fills and more endears
The silence when a bird hath ceased to sing.

FOR THE FIRST PAGE OF THE ALBUM.

I OPEN this to write for her
　Within whose gates is ever Peace;
Beneath whose roof the wanderer
　Finds from his wayside cares release.

Her presence is in every room,
　Her silent love is everywhere,
As pleasant as a soft perfume,
　As soothing as a twilight air.

No song shall tell the friendly debt
　My gratitude were glad to pay;
But here may other singers set
　The half of what I fain would say.

More sweetly may their songs be made,
　Their lines in purer cadence fall,
Yet none — yet none leaves more unsaid,
　With truer wish to say it all.

September 10. 1883.

98

FAREWELL TO SALVINI.[1]

APRIL 26TH, 1883.

ALTHOUGH a curtain of the salt sea-mist
    May fall between the actor and our eyes—
  Although he change for dear and softer skies
These that the sun has yet but coyly kissed—
Although the voice to which we loved to list
    Fail ere the thunder of our plaudits dies—
  Although he parts from us in gracious wise,
With grateful memory left his eulogist—
  His best is with us still.

                    His perfect art
  Has held us 'twixt a heart-throb and a tear—
    Cheating our souls to passionate belief.
And in his greatness we have now some part—
  We have been courtiers of the crownless Lear,
    And partners in Othello's mighty grief.

ON READING A POET'S FIRST BOOK.

THIS is a breath of summer wind
   That comes—we know not how—that goes
As softly,—leaving us behind
   Pleased with a smell of vine and rose.

Poet, shall this be all thy word?
   Blow on us with a bolder breeze;
Until we rise, as having heard
   The sob, the song of far-off seas.

Blow in thy shell until thou draw,
   From inner whorls where still they sleep,
The notes unguessed of love and awe,
   And all thy song grow full and deep.

Feeble may be the scanty phrase —
   Thy dream a dream tongue never spake —
Yet shall thy note, through doubtful days,
   Swell stronger for Endeavor's sake.

As Jacob, wrestling through the night,
   Felt all his muscles strengthen fast
With wakening strength, and met the light
   Blessèd and strong, though overcast.

FEMININE.

SHE might have known it in the earlier Spring,
  That all my heart with vague desire was stirred;
And, ere the Summer winds had taken wing,
  I told her; but she smiled and said no word.

The Autumn's eager hand his red gold grasped,
  And she was silent; till from skies grown drear
Fell soft one fine, first snow-flake, and she clasped
  My neck and cried, "Love, we have lost a year!"

REDEMPTION.

AS to the drunkard who at morn doth wake
    Are the clear waters of the virgin spring
Wherewith he bathes his eyes that burn and sting
And his intolerable thirst doth slake,
So is the thought of thee to me, who break
   One sober moment, sick and shuddering,
   From all my life's unworthiness, to fling
Me at thy memory's feet, and for Love's sake
Pray that thy peace may enter in my soul.
   Love, thou hast heard! My veins more calmly flow—
    The madness of the night is passed away—
Fire of false eyes, thirst of the cursèd bowl—
   I drink deep of thy purity, and lo !
    Thou hast given me new heart to meet the day.

TRIUMPH.

THE dawn came in through the bars of the
blind,—
And the winter's dawn is gray,—
And said — However you cheat your mind,
The hours are flying away.

A ghost of a dawn, and pale and weak —
Has the sun a heart, I said,
To throw a morning flush on the cheek
Whence a fairer flush has fled?

As a gray rose-leaf that is fading white
Was the cheek where I set my kiss;
And on that side of the bed all night
Death had watched, and I on this.

I kissed her lips, they were half apart,
Yet they made no answering sign;
Death's hand was on her failing heart,
And his eyes said — " She is mine."

ULTIMA THULE.

I set my lips on the blue-veined lid,
  Half-veiled by her death-damp hair;
And oh, for the violet depths it hid,
  And the light I longed for there!

Faint day and the fainter life awoke,
  And the night was overpast;
And I said — "Though never in life you spoke,
  Oh, speak with a look at last!"

For the space of a heart-beat fluttered her breath,
  As a bird's wing spread to flee;
She turned her weary arms to Death,
  And the light of her eyes to me.

TO HER.

PERCHANCE the spell that now must part
    Our lives may yet be broken ;
And then your sweet unconscious heart
    May know my love unspoken.
Perchance the jealous seal of Time
    May break in some far season;
And you will read this book of rhyme,
    And know the rhyme's dear reason.

How long ago the song began !
    How lonely was the singer,
Whose mistress never thought to scan
    The lines he dared to bring her !
Oh, will you ever read it true,
    When all the rhymes are ended —
How much of Hope, of Love, of You,
    With every verse was blended.

Who knows?   But when the bars shall fall
    That set our souls asunder,
May you, at last, in hearing all,
    Feel Love grow out of Wonder;
And may the song be glad as when
    The boy's fresh voice commenced it ;
And may my heart be beating then,
    To feel your own against it !

NOTES.

1 " There was a vague murmur in the air of little brooks, that one might fancy had lost their way in the darkness, and were whispering together how they should get home."

————" In the Distance," by G. P. Lathrop.

2 The only authority I have for calling this "A Real Romance" is the following, clipped from a stray newspaper in '77 or '78 :

"A school-girl at Bellefontaine, Ohio, offended her boy lover, and he refused to speak to her. She passed a note to him, asking forgiveness, but he refused. She wrote to him again, saying that she would kill herself if he did not make up ; and he replied that he would be glad to go to her funeral. She then began her suicidal efforts by drinking a bottle of red ink, which only made her sick. A bottle of black ink had no deadlier effect. Finally, she cut her throat with a knife, but not fatally, though she made a deep and dangerous gash."

3 Like the Roman citizen's right of appeal to Cæsar, there was, according to some authorities, a supreme right of appeal to Harold of Normandy. It was invoked by crying " Haro! Haro ! Haro !" In a modified form, the legal tradition still survives, I believe, in some of the Channel Islands.

4 Read at the farewell dinner to Salvini, New-York, April 26th, 1883.